William Watson Turnbull

Inebriae, Legend of Wyoma Lake, and Other Poems

William Watson Turnbull

Inebriae, Legend of Wyoma Lake, and Other Poems

ISBN/EAN: 9783337393359

Printed in Europe, USA, Canada, Australia, Japan

Cover: Foto ©Andreas Hilbeck / pixelio.de

More available books at **www.hansebooks.com**

INEBRIÆ,

LEGEND OF WYOMA LAKE,

AND

OTHER POEMS.

BY

WILLIAM WATSON TURNBULL.

———————

BOSTON:

ALFRED MUDGE & SON, PRINTERS.

1871.

CONTENTS.

RELIGIOUS POEMS.

INEBRIÆ.

INEBRIÆ.

I MMORTAL beings, bend your list'ning ears !
   While passing through this veil of woe and tears,
From pratt'ling youth to hoary-headed age,
We act immortal scenes, — this earth 's the stage ;
And every act of body or of mind
Will leave a good or evil wake behind.
What need we, then, to guard our thoughts and ways ;
To walk with caution, softly, all our days ;
Lest in the fatal paths of sin we tread,
And therein, guileless, others captive lead ?
We voyage on the noble river, Time,
Beneath, around, above, are themes sublime ;
Within, a vessel freighted with desire ;
Without, are tempters luring to inspire
Our sinful passions with a sinful zeal
For pleasures false, that mar the spirit's weal,
And draw our souls from virtue's honored bower,
To scenes of madness with Satanic power.
Behold ! on either side the mossy lawn,
Beneath whose verdant shade volcanoes yawn ;

Here is the painted temptress, there the shrine
To Mammon, or some god yet not divine.
To mention all the errors that estrange
The soul from good, and noble minds derange,
However fervent the desire or will,
Is equally beyond our aim and skill.
Yet there's a rock, or island, near the main,
Where Bacchus holds unenviable reign.
To picture forth some scenes upon his realm,
To pierce the veil his subjects overwhelm,
Or point deliverance, will be our task ; —
And for this end your patience would we ask.

'T is thus we find thee out, death-dealing cup ;
Who sit with thee but dire confusion sup.
Alas! what tinctured thoughts to thee we trace ;
To thee ascribe what want of heavenly grace.
How few with safety can thy chalice touch ?
How many taste thee, but again to clutch ?
Who find that moderation 's but the spark
That wakes the slumb'ring efforts of the shark,
Or falls upon a magazine of sin,
That rages with sad tumults high within.
How can we pray, "lead not to tempter's sway,"
Or seek aright the great salvation's way,
When trifling with the fire that curst the sot,
And is, to pure desire, the antidote ?
How often is our purest, happiest hour,
Changed to degrading thoughts when in thy power,

When we to commune with our God aspire,
To converse with the devil by thy fire?
Behold! thy birth midst emblems of that state
In which thy conquered are assigned their fate;
In dungeon's darkness lies fermenting there,
Where stifling fumes arise to taint the air,
Like smoke, the dismal, dark'ning glooms emit,
Where Satan with his demon angels sit.
Then passing through a hideous, loathsome worm,
What trickling sound comes from its serpent form?
Reminds us of the worm that never dies,
But gnawing, gnawing, yet in silence lies.
Those vessels which with liquid fires are drenched,
Warn of the fire that never shall be quenched.
Behold! what heaps of wasted cereals lie,
Fit only for the muck-heap or the sty.
Thus strong and countless are thy thousands slain,
Yet erring nature turns to thee again.
'T were well that men this poison'd nest unearth,
Destroy the eggs, and crush thee in thy birth.
Thou charming serpent, Satan's deepest wile!
Thy fangs are piercing, whilst thine eyes beguile.
Who seek thine aid to banish grief or woe,
With every draught a double grief will sow.
Thy sparkling cup for fancied joys they wring,
And deeply drink, but with the dregs thy sting.
Thy sting is felt, but, like the moth to light,
They turn to revel with returning night;
And nightly revel, as they sing, or tell

Their song, or story, newly raked from hell.

Again the moth has touched the light that lures,

Though every touch a horrid fate insures;

The feath'ry wool, from which it comfort found,

Flies off, is singed, and scattered all around.

Thus man his substance wastes to feed the flame,

His appetite for folly, sin, and shame.

Back to the light again, his limbs are burned,

For every warning of the past is spurned.

And now degraded nature bites the dust,

As he from door to door in shame is thrust;

Till met by some kind, philanthropic heart,

Who sees his state, and, pitying, takes his part:

To lift him up, to ransom from the grave, —

For where there's life there's hope the lost to save.

With noble flutter of his wings, he's up,

And surely, now, will never touch the cup;

Yet still around the dazzling light he flies,

Till, writhing, scorch'd, in anguish falls and dies?

Nay, lives, to tread the dungeon's deepest path,

And drink forever of the cup of wrath.

Oh! deep, humiliating sight to see!

Such noble limb of nature's noblest tree

A rigid corpse, a bloated suicide!

From which humanity, ashamed, would hide.

A noble image of his God thus torn,

The good man's pity, but the wicked's scorn.

O, erring man! wouldst thou not fly anon,

With fleetest step, and fear thy heart dethrone,

To hear the rattle of the snake in grass ?
Fly, then, the rattle of the gathering glass
To fill anew ; but drink, and on thy tomb
Read this : " Another glass has sealed my doom."
Fly ! for the rattlesnake, prepared to strike,
Hath raised itself, and with its fevered spike
Thy soul will pierce ; for he who wields the power
Seeks both thy soul and body to devour.
Fly, then, the glittering haunts of vice,
The teeming halls of Satan's strong device !
Wilt thou not hear the voice of wisdom call
To thee, to those thy drinking comrades, all ?
The arrow, poison-tipp'd, is on the wing,
That brings thee captive to the Sulphur King.
Then, midst thy dissipation, sit thee still,
And with the reeling tosspot drink thy fill.
But, as thou raisest high the burning cup,
If conscience be not yet quite dead, look up !
See yonder grim and ghastly spectre, Death !
Behold his frown, and, trembling, hold thy breath, —
By thee invited, yet unwelcome guest ;
With balanced dart, and pointed for thy breast,
See, how he waits the moment of his power,
With lipless teeth, and greedy to devour !
Behold him watching as you raise the bowl,
To creep another footstep near thy soul ;
His hands uplifted, with triumphant spleen,
And through those eyeless sockets victory seen,
As on *thee*, fixed, his steady stare he keeps,

But, o'er thy chair, thy guardian angel weeps!
Yes, weeps! Because her charge is lost in sin,
And soon must see his endless doom begin, —
Who at thy birth had hailed thee, undefiled,
And o'er thy cradled innocence had smiled!
Who all thy youth had guarded thee from harm,
And threw around thy soul life's brightest charm!
Who shielded thee by day, who watched by night,
And filled thy couch with visions of delight!
She weeps! weeps, for a gem is lost to Heaven!
Weeps o'er a soul by self to Satan given.
Oh, wouldst thou comfort yet this thing of light?
Up! up! and with thy utmost strength and might,
Seize the dread cup with firm and steady aim,
Ere death advance to cover thee with shame!
And hurl it at his head, while yet you may
Cheat the grim tyrant of untimely prey!
And turn thee to that form, who mourned above;
She yet will bear thee on the wings of love
To virtue's ever-green and pleasant field,
Where Hope grows bright, and leans on Faith, her shield.

O Virtue, pure and sweet, harmonious sound!
Thy softest amours are with olive crowned;
Thine is the path of pleasure's sweetest joy,
And thine the cup of bliss without alloy!
Of thine intrinsic beauty would I sing,
And to thy comeliness would homage bring;
Thrice happy household fraught with love to thee,

Where all to sing thy praise in love agree.

Can brightest fancy from her noblest store,

In fairy ramblings culled from shore to shore,

Produce a nobler love-inspiring sight?

Sweet children, leaping with a fond delight,

To meet their father coming from his toil,

And round his limbs their lovely arms they coil;

Their rosy, dimpled faces, beaming mirth,

Or smiles of tribute to sweet virtue's worth;

Their glossy ringlets floating in the air,

And sunbeams playing through their golden hair.

See how he stoops to print on each the kiss, —

A perfect picture of a perfect bliss.

Then, clasping each a hand, they onward move,

In dancing rivalry, their love to prove,

And eager tell the stories of the day, —

Strange things that happened in their walks or play.

The welkin round with merry laughter rings,

Which to the cottage door the mother brings;

Who, glad, receives the tender, sweet embrace,

Returned by her with modesty and grace.

Already are the little busy bees

Loud telling "Papa's come!" on grandpa's knees,

Who thoughtful sat, now rouses from his muse,

And strokes them kindly for the welcome news.

Then round the table, groaning 'neath its weight

Of cheering social comforts, all are sate.

The little ones, by godly parents trained,

Bow low their heads, with reverence unfeigned;

With pious, open hand, and closed eye,
The aged patriarch sends up on high
The words of praise and thanks for mercies past,
The present blest, such bounties long may last.
And ever may all gifts, in mercy sent,
Flow through the everlasting covenant ;
Then all the satisfying viands sup,
And drink the cheering, warm, appeasing cup.
The table cleared, some gentle work and toys,
Or songs and tunes, a pleasant hour employs.
The father, joining in the children's sports,
With hum'rous fables their affection courts ;
The youthful mother, — overjoyed to see
Her household filled with happiness and glee, —
To laugh at papa's wit, her knitting stays,
While with the clew the well-fed kitten plays.
Or grandpa tells some stories of his youth,
With pointed moral, as a guide to truth.
Now toys and all aside with care are laid,
And vows around the family altar paid ;
With holy rev'rence due, the father leads,
For pardoning and helping grace he pleads,
That He, who all their daily wants supplies,
Would now accept their evening sacrifice,
And would vouchsafe his holy presence there,
That each alike this sacred joy may share.
Infused on all, the flaming tongues descend,
Their hearts with burning fervor high ascend ;
With swelling pathos from their lips are rolled

The sweet commingling notes of young and old,
In tones of sacred praise, both loud and long,
That mount to mingle with the angels' song.
Then from the Sacred Volume, with delight,
Are read the records of Jehovah's might, —
How He the heathen nations did subdue,
And all the enemies of Israel slew ;
Or led them captive, by his sovereign grace, —
Captives to freedom and eternal peace.
Together, kneeling down before the throne
Of grace, their cares and wants are all made known,
In solemn accents, by the hoary sage,
Whose earnest supplications all engage.
And God is praised for faithfulness each night,
And mercies new as comes the morning light.
For each a prayer : now, all the household blest,
On relatives and friends like blessings rest ;
Their town, their country, and their nation's cause,
That all may live submissive to God's laws ;
All nations and all ranks of men embraced,
Who dwell on land, or plow the ocean's waste ;
That all into the fold of Him who died
Be brought, and through his blood be sanctified ;
That all iniquity may cease, all lands be pure,
Ascribing praise and glory to endure.
Down from the mount, each face with radiance fair,
On papa's knees the children raise their prayer
In sweet simplicity. Then, fondly kissed,
They and their grandsire now retire to rest.

2

The youthful, loving parents left alone,
To intercourse and sweet communings prone,
Breathe out their love in sympathy of heart,
And each to other's bliss anew impart.
O, hallowed hour! where love is unestranged,
Each thought unbosomed, hearts anew exchanged,
In wrapt embrace, their ecstasies the same,
And tender pressures feed the glowing flame!
Oh, moments freighted with unmingled bliss!
Can sordid musings taste a joy like this?
The luscious fruit, from virtue's vine so ripe,
Of which e'en wooing days are but a type;
No false inspiring stimulant they need
From Bacchus' fiery cup or honey'd mead;
Their joys spring teeming from the inmost soul,
And, like the snowballs, gather as they roll.
Their cares divided, and their joys combined,
They seek from books improvement for the mind;
Or, he had bought the papers by the way,
From which he reads the topics of the day, —
The strange vicissitudes of poor, or great,
Or what is passing in the church or state;
Or now, with awe, some tidings from afar,
Of nations merged in fierce and bloody war;
Or kingdoms, long at strife, agree to cease,
And o'er their groaning lands proclaim a peace.
Again, the sympathetic tear is shed
O'er some poor prodigal reported dead,
As thoughts revert to homes made desolate,

And parents wrapped in woe, disconsolate.

In union rise their hearts in silent prayer,

That God would save *their* homes from such despair ;

That light divine be to their children given,

To show that virtue is the path to heaven ;

That wisdom be their guide to purity,

To glory, honor, immortality ;

That when they meet the tempter in the world,

The banner of the cross by them unfurled,

May fright the roaring lion from his prey,

And lead them safe through all that would betray.

Alas, reported dead ! gone to the grave,

Beyond the reach of hope or power to save !

Him had they known, in childhood gambol free,

To chase the butterfly across the lea ;

While from his very feet the lark upsprang,

And o'er his head with joyous warblings sang,

For nature hath an instinct given to all,

To judge between the innocent's and guilty's call ;

To know the prattling feet and lightsome air,

From creeping treachery and fowler's snare.

But, see ! the child had left his harmless play,

To venture on pursuits in danger's way ;

The humming of a bee allured his eyes,

And after it with nimble step he hies ;

Sees it alight upon a blushing rose,

An inward longing for its honey grows.

With silent step he nears the fragrant bush,

And, cap in hand, he aims a sudden push ;

Now mark the look his rueful face adorns, —
He feels the sting, and falls among the thorns.
Ah! thus was he in after years betrayed,
When he to chase the phantom Pleasure strayed;
With youths profane, he wandered to the bar,
Where learning is unlearnt and virtue far;
Or gambled in the banks of faro fame,
And lost his golden chips at keno game.
The oft-repeated glass his reason maze;
His passions fire, and he, with wanton gaze,
Saw vice upon a bed of roses lie, —
Ran to embrace; embracing, cast the die.
Thorns in his path, his flesh, and in his heart
He sowed, till to his liver strikes the dart.
To drown remorse, again the cup he seized;
With lust revived and guilty conscience eased,
Alternately, from vice to vice he turned,
Till death ensued from fires his vitals burned.
Oh, cup of death! what multitudes increase,
Whom thou hast slain; where will thy ravage cease?
Come, see what desolation thou hast made,
Thou fell invader of the peaceful shade!
On pleasant groves, where lovers sought to meet,
And friendly schoolmates wooed the soft retreat;
Where warblers sang their sweetest melodies,
Where flowers exhaled perfumes of paradise,
And gentle zephyrs whispered, — nature's pleased.
Thy wanton, sacrilegious hands have seized,
Till o'er the choicest spots of woods and plains,

Where peace was found, now strife and discord reigns;
And brawling riot, with the hideous sound
Of oaths and cursing, fills the air around;
Till e'en the sweetest Sabbath-morning chime
Is mingled with the startling cry of crime,
Committed in the hidden, secret shade,
By gin-besotted minions of the glade.
Whilst half-oblivious parents in the wood
Sit tippling, heedless of their offspring's good.
Their honor, happiness, and virtue lost,
Ere yet departing childhood's line is crossed.
Come! I will charge thee with a motley throng
Of deeds of darkness, infamy, and wrong!
Of anger brew'd, and happy households filled
With tinctured guilt and misery distilled!
Nor are thy fearful ravages confined
To men of equal state or equal mind.
At palace hall and cot thy blow is dealt;
The ignorant and learned its power have felt.
See! at thy touch the head of genius bow,
The laurel wither on the poet's brow!
Strong science, basely crawling in the dust,
A drivelling idiot and slave of lust!
Yet high we raise the voice, to lift the veil,
And follow hard upon the dismal trail;
To tell of nations ruined by thy blight,
Or hovels filled with woe, — a ghastly sight.
See the proud conqueror of a world subdued!
Great Alexander, riotous and drunken viewed!

Intoxication crowns his sullied fame,

And doomed Persepolis, through wasting flame,

A blackened monument to folly stands

In stately columns high, in Persia's land!

The cup again his deadly passion fires,

And by his hand his noblest friend expires;

With anguish and remorse, the sages tell,

His bosom heaved when faithful Clitus fell.

Behold Palmyra's princes in the field,

Unwearied face the foe with sword and shield;

Who braves the dangers of the hottest fray,

And fearless leads her soldiers all the day.

Praised by the nations for her chastity,

And by the lieges for her constancy;

Yet for her deep intoxication's blamed,

By wine so easy conquered and defamed.

What steeled the traitor's heart, and nerved his arm

To treacherous deeds, that scatter'd dread alarm

O'er all the land, and caused by the blow,

Not one, but every nation's tears to flow?

That sent through all the earth the pang of grief,

As if each nation lost an honored chief?

Oh, Lincoln, great and good, we mourn thy doom!

The heart of every true man is thy tomb;

There shalt thou rest embalmed, whilst ages roll,

The honored tenant of each grateful soul;

Thy laurel crown, forever green and new,

With tears all generations shall bedew.

Thus wine has made a nation's tears to flow,
And stamped oppression on a monarch's brow.
This, this, the sin that stained Zenobia,
And draped thy statues, fair Columbia!

Now view the city's desolate domains;
The dismal shelter of the drunken trains;
In garret, or in filthy cellar stowed,
Promiscuous hordes of males and females, bowed
With misery, despair, disease, and death,
And poisoned air, inhaled with every breath.
The tiny, sickly, drooping, infant form,
Bare food for life, less clothes to keep it warm,
Who nestles on a mother's wither'd breast,
Is beat, for wailing, by the inhuman pest.
Or, look beyond, — upon a bed of reeds,
Where chill winds blow, and fell consumption feeds,
A gentle maiden, shiv'ring in the cold,
Once beautiful, now prematurely old;
And through the single, threadbare cover seen
How poor her form, emaciate and lean.
She, once a father's only joy, so fair,
And a once tender mother's only care.
And later, when the serpent round them coiled,
And drove them forth, how earnestly she toiled;
By day, by night, how swift her needle sped,
To save from death, to bring them daily bread!
And, oh, how earnestly to God she cried,
To turn them from their ways, with sin so dyed!

(For she had early learned the vital breath ;
Her only comfort now in hour of death.)
How deeply bleeds that tender, loving soul,
To see them nearing still the drunkard's goal ;
And yet, for drink, they from her limbs will tear
Each comfort mourning charity may bear ;
Nor piteous look, nor agonizing tear,
Can move their demon hearts, so hard and sear.
Wasted with sorrow, hardship, toil, and care,
Thus sinking, fades a form so young and fair ;
With faith in God, by every pang increased,
Her ling'ring spirit waits to be released ;
Till wafted up on high, on angels' wings,
Triumphant songs of praise forever sings, —
A sweet young flower, with garbage (near entombed)
Cast forth, but yet amidst corruption bloomed ;
Plucked by a kind and gentle hand away
From gloomy putrefaction and decay
To bloom in gardens of celestial light,
Amidst the flowers of heaven's choice delight.
But, hark ! what shriek is that ? what flurried strife ?
A reeling madman strikes his tender wife,
Who, trembling, oft besought him to abstain,
And now had feebly striven to detain
Him forth from wand'ring with a golden toy,
But the last relic of their household's joy.
The blow is dealt ; a first but fatal blow,
For he had loved her who is now brought low.
Amazed ! bewildered ! filled with stupid awe !

Surrounded! seized by officers of law!
He finds himself a murderer, self-condemned,
By heaven and earth detested and contemned;
His children doomed to vagrancy and want,
On whom the world will ceaseless cast the taunt;
His children's children still will bear the stain,
Which generations whisper back again.
Oh, friends, awake! be warnéd, and beware
The serpent's sting, the fowler's hidden snare.
Art thou inthralled, and dost thou feel alarm?
Thou canst not, of thyself, break Satan's charm.
Seek grace divine; go seek it, even now,
And wipe those sweat-drops from thy fever'd brow.
Omnipotence alone can break the spell,
And lead again with innocence to dwell.
Dreadst thou the consequences of past sins?
Here, then, the influence of grace begins.
Wouldst thou in deep despair thyself impale?
With mercy infinite thou shalt not fail;
The childlike cry, the feebly uttered groan,
Make sin and Satan tremble on their throne.
The fountain open'd up on Calvary's hill
Can cleanse the soul and purify the will;
However deep the wound sin's sting hath made,
There's victory for thee, — thy ransom's paid.
Then to thy lips this living water raise,
'T is this will cheer thy life through brighter days.

LEGEND

OF

WYOMA LAKE.

LEGEND OF WYOMA LAKE.

FAIR Wyoma, thy peaceful gleam
    Disturbs not now a bride's sweet dream
        So rapturous ;
Yet have thy waves been scenes of strife,
When tomahawk and scalping-knife
        Were venturous.

Long years ago, when pilgrims came
To find a refuge, and proclaim
        The Christian faith,
There settled, near to Lynn's High Rock,
A pastor with his humble flock ;
        Behold, he pray'th !

Then Pastor, people, all unite,
With honest hardihood and might,
        In sweat and toil,
To form the log, to clear the ground,
To build their log hut on the mound,
        And till the soil.

Peace reigned supreme in this retreat,
When friendship, toil, and rest were sweet,
      They dwelt in love.
Though driven from his native home,
The Christian's peace, where'er he roam,
      Is from above.

Through summer's bloom and winter's gray
The old were calm, the children gay
      In playfulness.
And youthful wooers met as now,
To whisper love 'neath yonder brow,
      In truthfulness.

It chanced, one brilliant, dappled morn,
A stalwart youth, with face unshorn,
      Yet not uncouth,
Stood forth before the altar's hue,
With a fair maid, whose eyes of blue
      Seemed liquid truth.

In holy wedlock joined they stand,
By their good shepherd's lifted hand,
      Are blessed anew;
And issue forth, in robes of white,
To a new world of life and light,
      In Hymen's view.

The bridegroom, mindful of his bride,
Had well provided, for a ride,
    Their wedding tour.
A dampness settled on her brow,
She felt, nor knew she why or how,
    Yet insecure.

Forth set the party, joyous, free, —
Left all behind them filled with glee,
    For happy days, —
To Wyoma's fair lake ; there dine
Upon its marge ; return ere shine
    The moon's pale rays.

Thus purposed they ; and reach the lake,
Through tangled wood and ferny brake
    Interminable.
And merrily rang the woods that day,
And merrily did the waters say,
    Be sociable.

Ah, Wyoma ! not as thou art,
Of former years thou'rt but a part ;
    Thy waters few.
Then was thy margin widely spread,
Nor boat, nor path across thee led,
    Save the canoe.

A terror then to civilized,
Who were by savages despised,
           And massacred.
Wild hordes around thy banks defiled,
And through thee swam the reindeer mild,
           And ant'lered.

In solitude thy mirror'd face
Reflective shed, in tranquil grace,
           The trees and skies ;
And on thy limpid wave wild flocks
Were seen, amongst the reeds and rocks,
           To sink and rise.

The bridal party here prepare
Their social meal, of dainty fare,
           Upon the grass,
While bride and bridegroom quietly seek —
Unknown to them, a lover's freak —
           Some hidden pass.

Unconscious wanderers ! stop and think !
The path you tread 's a dang'rous brink
           To certain ruin ;
For, ere you know it, you may meet,
Waked by the twig-break 'neath your feet,
           Savage or bruin.

Still wander they, unconscious pair!
The first lone wedded hours are fair
                Forgetfulness ;
They, only they, who taste can tell
Their mystic sweets, or picture well
                Their happiness.

Quick as the hawk upon its prey,
Or like the flashing meteor's ray,
                The stealthy blow
Falls heavily ; and on the ground
Lies bleeding, e'en without sound,
                Our hero low ;

And, like a stricken fawn, his bride
Falls, dumb and senseless, by his side,
                Without a wound.
She saw her husband-lover down,
She saw the painted Indian's frown,
                And helpless swooned.

An easy prey, to bind and bear
Them forth triumphantly, to where
                Lay his frail bark.
So noiselessly he lays them, bound,
In his canoe, that not a sound,
                Or e'en a mark,

Is on the water, as he laves
Its face, and laps its gentle waves
                    Beneath the bushes ;
Till, far off on the other side,
Beneath a tree, whose branches wide
                    Aside he pushes.

And on the sward his light canoe,
With scarcely living freight, he drew, ·
                    With blood-stained hands ;
He, from the woods, is joined by one,
Red-skinned and painted.   Still anon
                    Come other bands,

Who hail their chief, and bear away
Their helpless victims, as they lay
                    Insensible.
And soon the camping ground is reached,
And soon the wigwams' sides are breached
                    Defensible.

Her bonds removed, they lay apart,
'Midst trophies wild of savage art,
                    To die or languish ;
Fair wind-spread locks her face conceal,
'Neath which, pale furrowed marks reveal
                    Her spirit's anguish.

The merry bridal party wait
Their coming; sportive say, " They 're late ;
           They still are wooing."
Or, " Wanting lessons still of love,
" Have gone to seek the turtle-dove,
           And will come cooing."

But some, who feared, their fears reveal ;
With solemn awe each lip is sealed
           In painful musing ;
Of negligence, that left to stray,
Unarmed, unhelped, in dang'rous way,
           Each self-accusing.

With heavy, anxious hearts they search
From place to place, in every perch,
           And loud they hollow.
'T was vain ! the wild woods' echo came,
Clear and responsive, to the name,
           Yet none to follow.

A youth, more venturesome than most,
And near related to the lost,
           Came back in haste ;
He 'd seen the gory glade, where fell
His friend ; and, to the lake, too well
           The blood had traced.

Death-like, oppressive silence palls,
Marred only by the leaf that falls
                    In circling course ;
To action ! one must bear the news.
Most fit, the witness, to accuse,
                    And raise a force.

Homeward ! with sob and aching breast,
The grief-bowed maids, so joyous dressed,
                    This youth their guide.
The others, mourning left, prepare
Great rafts to cross the lake so fair,
                    By moonlight tide.

Homeward ! all nature seemed to mourn,
And through the forest trees was borne
                    The wind's deep sigh.
Like a dread pall, mists onward sail,
To feed the dripping leaves, and veil
                    The cloud-draped sky.

Home ! but, alas, what heavy groans
From every cot reveal in tones
                    The heart's sad throb !
Parents, who joined their children hale,
Now join in one their piteous wail
                    And fitful sob.

With weapons new, or old and rusty,
Forth sped a numerous band, and trusty,
   To join their fellows.
But when the turbid lake is made,
The rain sweeps fast, the lightnings played,
   And thunder bellows.

Like heavy, drooping lead, their hearts
Down sink, as pierced with darts
   In painful fray.
Are Heaven and earth 'gainst them combined?
All night, through darkness, rain, and wind,
   They watch and pray.

She first to consciousness awakes
In horror ; and, convulsive, shakes
   Her gentle frame,
As round her dance, in hideous form,
The tribe, with monstrous yell and storm, —
   Their fiercest game.

The sun midst blackened clouds descends ;
Their feasting and their prancing ends
   In council deep,
Where death, and worse than death's decreed!
Then some go forth ; the rest, with speed,
   Prepare to sleep.

In trembling contemplation, she
Feigned all unconscious still to be,
            To those around ;
In dread suspense, till all their number,
From youth to age, seem lost in slumber,
            Both deep and sound.

She stirs ; so does a savage near her ;
In every move he seemed to hear her,
            And start, awake ;
Thus hemmed, she, looking round, espies
Her low-laid mate, whose heavy sighs
            Her heart will break.

Heaven helps when earthly sources fail,
Nor all the hosts of hell prevail, —
            Against His feeble.
Dark lowered the sky, ere forth the chief
On other errand dark with grief,
            And full of evil,

Had wandered, to return in might
And lustfulness, ere depth of night,
            His purpose, what ?
The gath'ring storm comes on apace,
With angry menace in its face,
            Destruction fraught.

Gleam, gleam, the lightning's lurid flash!
'Mid thunder's awful roll and crash,
   With wind and deluge;
Till back and forth the wigwams swayed,
Like ships in storm with anchor stayed,
   Put in for refuge.

Fast speak the Indians, now awake,
While seemed the earth beneath to shake,
   With trembling rage;
And motion quick, to bind anew
Their captive; lest the storm that blew
   Should all engage.

But ere the withes to bind are ready,
The raging wind, with whirling eddy,
   Their wigwams whisk!
Confused, both tents and savage mingle;
With thunders' roar their ears still tingle,
   And fire flashed brisk.

Left for a moment, thus, alone!
She marked the spot, when lightning shone,
   Where lay her lord;
And quick, through darkness, ere the glares
Reveal her act, she lifts and bears
   Her heavy ward.

Fear lent her courage, joy lent strength;
The lightnings showed the path the length,
　　　　Till near the lake;
There, sinking, faints beneath the load,
And failed her all that seemed to goad
　　　　Her onward wake.

But, hark! aloft the eagles scream;
She wakes, as from an evil dream,
　　　　Midst drenching rain;
And with her burden to the boat,
Swift as the roe, or mountain goat,
　　　　Nor feeling pain.

'Twas but a moment; quick the bark
Is skimming o'er the waters dark
　　　　And perilous;
While by the lightning 'lumined skies
Are seen the Indians' glaring eyes,
　　　　So hideous.

Fast by the driving storm they toss
Upon the lake, till near across,
　　　　Without or paddle;
And now, as lifeless, on his breast
She falls. Caught in the reeds, they rest,
　　　　As in a cradle,

Till purple dawn's pale rays came creeping
In the far East, to wake the sleeping,
>> As from the dead.
Full fair, her white robes windward played,
And on her bosom, resting, laid
>> A blood-stained head.

Thus beautiful — a snow-white hand
Curved o'er head — the weary band
>> Of seekers found them ;
And, like a fleecy cloud escaped,
The thin, uplifting mist had shaped
>> A halo round them.

So pleased, the searchers, to behold
Within the green and leafy fold
>> So tranquilly,
Leave them alone, through shine and storm,
That *all* may view this beauteous form,
>> Th' water-lily.

Still come the fairies every morn
To sprinkle with their dewy horn
>> The sweet, pale face.
Go mark the lake when dawn is shed,
The snow-white robe, the bleeding head,
>> In her embrace.

Not dead! but beautiful and fair;
Their fragrance scents the summer air
With balmy fume.
And year by year the Naiad keeps
Her watch o'er them, and on the deeps
Renews their bloom.

DR. JOTHAM TINDALE'S

CUE A CURE.

A LEGEND OF LYNN.

DR. JOTHAM TINDALE'S CUE A CURE.

A LEGEND OF LYNN.

———

'TIS some two hundred years ago
    Since Doctor Tindale lived below.
His pedigree, — though no one knows, —
'T is possible, the story goes
(For which we owe an obligation
To " Jewels of the third Plantation "),
That he could trace, from *him* descent,
Who wrote the English Testament.

    A little man, scarce five feet high ;
By no means stout, but very spry ;
A bony chin, and long, sharp nose ;
He wore broad shoes with turned-up toes ;
His scarlet stocking so bewitches !
Red ribbons tied his yellow breeches :
A bob-tailed coat, of bottle-green,
So tightly drawn, the buttons lean ;
The collar, half-way up his head,
An ample white one overspread ;

A jaunty hat, oft raised for thanks,
With which the wind played sportive pranks,
But which, when raised, disclosed to view
The ever-memorable cue.

This cue the Doctor idolized
With childish pride, though all disguised ;
Its composition was his hair
So stringent braced, his pelt might tear ;
This strain his eyes so wide would keep,
He must relieve, or never sleep.
The cue, bound by an eel-skin tie,
Projected horizontally ;
And, as its hue to ruddy tends,
Kept powdered to its knotted ends.
His brow, so sloping towards the cue,
Left doubtful where his knowledge grew ;
The chubby cheeks and little lips
Displayed extensive ivory tips.

This Doctor Jotham was a cure :
No doubt his medicines were pure.
The nauseous, huge, concocted doses,
Made all his patients stop their noses ;
But as he was a man of learning,
From Harvard, hailed as all discerning,
They swallowed eagerly his drink,
That seldom left them time to think.

A pleasant man was Doctor Tindale;
Sick children dandled on his spindle,
And would some pretty stories tell
Of boys, who loved his pills so well;
With older people, too, was welcome,
For lively talk he always dealt 'um.
So much good-nature mixed the cup,
He always kept their spirits up.
His feeling heart and soothing manners
Might be a plea for physic banners;
No one could charge him with neglecting
A patient's cause, howe'er perplexing;
Especially, when o'er the breeze
He scented beneficial fees.
Thus Doctor Tindale's fame was wide,
Extending o'er the country side,
Through which he daily might be seen,
Upon a white horse, tall and lean,
To fly, on mercy's errand bent,
Wherever succor might be lent, —
A scarlet tunic in the breeze,
And medicine from neck to knees.
His cures, through drugs or instrumental, —
Including surgical and dental, —
Were practised on the crazy noodle,
Fit-stricken cat, or petted poodle;
He chickens nursed in his meanders,
And often cured a horse of glanders.

And thus he chased the life pursuer,
Removing aches or cloggy cruor:
No wonder Doctor Jotham boasts
Amazing cures in mighty hosts.

But here we have a pretty kettle, —
A case that tried his utmost metal;
In which, if drugs *did* fail, he sure
At once proclaimed his cue a cure.
One Aaron Rhodes lay sick and painful
With sore disease, acute and baneful;
A heated, tickling, vexing mote
Soon formed an abscess in his throat,
That put a stop to all vocation,
And threatened death by suffocation.
The Doctor every nerve did strain
To find a remedy — in vain.
For with the swelling swift encroaching,
He saw the crisis fast approaching.
In vain he every scheme resolved,
With pointed lance, or drugs dissolved;
Or strove to break by squeeze or rubbing,
Or giving Rhodes a healthy drubbing;
Or sought to find some antidote
By gazing down the afflicted throat,
In nervous agitation, crying,
"There's no occasion for your dying!"
He paced the floor, with head askew,
While points on high the trembling cue;

But still his brain gives no dictation
To ward the fatal termination.

'Tis Sunday night; the tumor gains;
An almost perfect silence reigns.
No breeze to make the windows rattle,
Nor e'en the fire sends out a crackle,
But gives a stifled, smould'ring heat,—
The Rhodés family burning peat,—
The patient's hard, uneasy breathing,
Alone is heard, as he lay seething.
The prim nurse by the fireside sat,
And nodded to the gray house-cat,
Reposing on an easy cushion,
Which now would rise to its ablution;
And then would stretch itself, and, gaping,
Resume again its dreams and napping.
Between them, in a big arm-chair,
The doctor sat with solemn air,
The all-beloved cue, so stable,
Projecting o'er the little table
That stood behind, with scores of phials,
Of which the tallow dip made dials;
Whilst round it, as a body-guard,
They formed, like veterans old and scarred.
The flame, by red, round spots bedimmed,
Might be revived, if slightly trimmed.
Soon Jotham, too, with vigils weary,
Began to nod; his eyes grew bleary,

4

And, notwithstanding his profession,
Nod soon chased nod in quick succession.
The cue stood sometimes at an angle,
Would sometimes 'mongst the bottles tangle,
As if 't would study all the labels,
And cure the man with Latin fables.
Again it would go, twitch and swishing,
As if engaged in earnest fishing, —
The fast succeeding jerks and quibbles,
Proclaim, at least, a lot of nibbles ;
But seeming weary thus to dandle,
Began to tantalize the candle.
Poor Aaron watched the curious bobbing,
And, though his throat with pain was throbbing,
He scarcely could contain a titter,
That filled his soul with pangs most bitter.
The easiest movement of a muscle
Would sting like life and death's last tussle.
A small tea-bell lay on the bed,
Quite handy to the patient's head ;
Which solemnly he thought to ring,
The nurse to his relief to bring ;
For if the cue's indulging fancies
Extended wide its comic dances,
A little more eccentric dafter,
Would, certain, cause his death of laughter ;
But, as he lay in mirthful thinking,
The solemn with the merry linking,

The Doctor's head quick backward came,
And forced the cue right in the flame.
When, lo!—O horror, flash and thunder!—
The cue, exploding, burst asunder
With such terrific noise and smoulder,
Near shook the head from off his shoulder.
Away went Doctor Joe's adorner
In singeing tufts through every corner;
Away went pussy, helter-skelter,
Below the trundle-bed for shelter;
Away went nurse beside her, squeezing,
Though neither could refrain from sneezing;
Away went Joe himself, still faster,
Upsetting phials, cups, and castor;
His elbows through the windows smashing,
His bare head bends the metal sashing,
Then up and down the room went skipping,
His nose with perspiration dripping;
His head oft clasping in his hands
To make him sure that still it stands.
The patient loud with laughter screamed;
The abscess broke, the matter streamed.
And after strangling, nothing grieved,
With flowing pus he felt relieved.
Thus burst the cue and burst the laughter,
And burst the stubborn tumor after;
And Aaron, like a flying ranger,
Was soon beyond the reach of danger.

For which, may endless thanks be due
To Doctor Tindale's fated cue.

The mystery we must explain —
Though learned men long tried in vain —
Of what had caused this great ado,
And saved Rhodes' life, but killed the cue.
The Doctor always went in state
To church or ceremonies great;
That morning, weighed with calls and care,
In which the busy household share,
He thought his lovely spouse he'd tell
The precious cue to powder well;
While he composed a potion neat
For Tawdy Jenkins' child so sweet.
This she had never done before,
But in perplexity she bore,
And, anxious that it should not want
For anything that she could vaunt,
Had passed the dredging-box in scorn,
And used the Doctor's powder-horn!

A RAMBLE

IN THE

GARDEN OF HOPE,

AND

OTHER POEMS.

A RAMBLE IN THE GARDEN OF HOPE.

IN ev'ry clime, in every age and station,
  Though Christian or a Brahmin be the nation,
Each has some bliss or promised good to follow,
However deep he in the mire may wallow.
As lights that flicker on the Ganges River,
Our Hope's faint glimm'rings in the heart still quiver.
When harsh and sterile winds, with chilling cold,
And withered leaves proclaim the summer old ;
Those wrecks of past delight, with sadness viewed,
In time shall have their freshness all renewed.
E'en in the darkest winter of the heart,
Some chirping robin in our path will start ;
Or, if too cold for out-of-doors, the storm
Drives man and beast to cot or stable warm ;
Those little warblers in the frost that welter,
Or perch upon our windows, seeking shelter,
Remind us that the feathered tribes of spring,
Whose sweetest notes still through our senses ring,
Though for a season winged their flight away,
Shall soon return to hold their matinée ;

So hope bespeaks, however deep entombed,
A more propitious spring than yet has bloomed.
The youth at school who fills the lowest place,
Hopes he may fill the highest yet with grace :
Nor do those visions fly on ent'ring college :
His aspirations rise to highest knowledge.
With midnight lamp laboriously he 'll pore,
To drink the soul of every book of lore.
And knowledge gained but fills with new desires,
To new discoveries now his soul aspires ;
And these, when made, but make him doubly bold,
To search again, and newer still unfold ;
Nor Newton, nor was Franklin yet content,
Till every inch of life they thus had spent.
Thus Herschel found beyond the galaxy,
With all its beauty, still a milky way.
The fight is now between those starry hopes,
And where to find the strongest telescopes.
See yonder busy author, undismayed
Alike by flooded field, or critic's blade,
Whate'er his subject, or how deep his theme,
Or high, or low, ambition lays his scheme ;
Sees, in his finished work, an honored name ;
His children's praises, or immortal fame.
Nor only of the magnates do we boast, —
We, petty scribblers, learn to hope the most,
Till disappointment checks our airy flight,
And turns our brilliant day to deepest night.

Yet will we scribble on, free, unconfined,
And cast our scatter'd fragments to the wind.
Some line may please the throng, or couplet brief,
As beauty shades the tinted autumn leaf;
And thus, though crowds contest the laurel's fate,
The poet still aspires to Laureate.
Where talent beams, ambition leads to fame,
And bent of mind will settle each his aim;
The nov'list, with perception of his race,
Tells their designs, their doings, mien, or grace.
Describe he virtue? admiration fills;
Or picture vice? the soul with horror thrills.
But history demands our higher praise,
And he who writes, a nobler call obeys;
For truth and knowledge he to all imparts,
Of nations, men, and manners, or the arts.
By Hope, through life, our every action's bent
To study, manufacture, or invent.
The peddler, too, whate'er his rags evince,
May be, for plodding, crowned a merchant prince.
E'en such a man of parts as Reuben Fickle,
Who acts at once whate'er his fancies tickle,
To sell a buyer, or attend his papers,
Is too much led away with whims and capers;
Too gay and merry now to act the clown,
And now too sober for a parson's gown.
In shifting element, is like the otter,
Whose life could not be long kept out of water;

And yet, when fortune smiles, and he can spin it,
Can't find his comfort lasting when he's in it;
Even he expects to wake some lovely morning,
In endless happiness, without much warning.
Hope sits enthroned in bliss, a fairy queen,
Whilst round her all our fond desires are seen.
Some laurels may be gained by one and all
Who stir themselves in answer to her call.

Love, like the ivy, clings on towers of hope,
And, climbing, shoots its branches o'er the top;
Will waving rise, 'mid tempest's rudest blast,
Though rivals press, or shadows overcast;
Dissolving Hope gives vigor to its life,
Which but reveals new ardor in the strife.
When Hope's high tower lies crumbling in the dust,
Love falls at last; but falls because it must.
Will crushed, midst ills and disappointments lie,
But 't is in anguish, for it cannot die.
O'er ruined hopes, its wounded tendrils stray,
To cover frailty or to mourn decay.

Once on a time, when fortune's favor smiled,
Olander, full of glee, the hours beguiled:
Love, joy, and beauty, all their force combined
To please, to tickle, and content his mind.
With loud professions round him, friendship pressed,
And all unite to call Olander blest.

A change disturbs the tenor of his dreams ;
His mind is now distracted with new themes.
That needful, yet all cause of trouble, money,
Like bee-bread, taints and spoils the purest honey ;
For sore adversity's keen blast now blows,
And all his plans in sad confusion throws ;
The gate of love, with sudden clang, is shut ;
The cords of friendship, falsely called, are cut ;
The voice of joy and gladness now is hushed,
And all that told of beauty now lies crushed ;
The heated winds of scandal blow disgrace
With venomed rancor in his careworn face.
For every former action fraught with good,
It finds an evil motive to intrude.
Olander senseless on the ground now lies,
While, from him, all the chaff of friendship flies ;
And oh how little of the genuine grain
Is left ; yet still enough to soothe his pain.
When consciousness to things of earth returns,
The flame of love still in his bosom burns ;
Sweet songs had cheered him in his darkest hour,
He dreamed those songs were from a loved one's bower.
"Those dreams," he cried, " and now, that voice I hear,
Betoken still her spirit hov'ring near."
The voice was that of love, and came more plain :
" Take courage, youth, your hopes are not in vain."
Nor love alone, but joy and beauty came,
And fortune, too, to crown his ardent aim ;

Thus, though the chilling wind of doubt and fear,
Like autumn blasts, make all things dull and sear,
The balmy breeze of hope will bring relief,
As roses spring with Summer's op'ning leaf.

Yet Hope is sometimes a deceptive snare,
And of her forms we caution to beware ;
For in her hand she holds to eager view,
Blessings unending, full enjoyed by few.
Invites to gardens of delicious fruit,
With cheering strains of dulcimer and lute ;
Where birds in joyous chorus sweetest sing,
And balmy zephyrs through the lichens ring ;
Where fragrant flowers with brilliant sunshine's gleam,
And willows bend to kiss the rippling stream ;
Enraptured, forth with hasty steps we hie,
To cull the flowers and taste the fruits we try.
Vain strife ! a mist comes thick'ning o'er our gaze,
And sadly leaves us in a piteous maze.
We stop in silent grief to wipe our eyes,
And strive to find where the deception lies ;
When, lo! we look again ; the mists dispel ;
Anew with hidden joys our bosoms swell,
For Hope again is seen with laden store
Of richer, brighter blessings than before ;
Invites again, and vows, for the delay,
Her best, her priceless treasures will repay.
Opening her book, she points, on every page,
To gladness and delights for youth and age.

Joys, strength renewed, we rise from darkest shades
To seize the blessing, but again it fades,
And leaves us piteously trembling o'er
With tenfold darker anguish than before.
When Hope's last flick'ring flame has quite gone out,
And thus, o'er Love, reigns darkness all about,
Its likeness still before our eyes will stand,
And fatal spell assumes in form, a hand,
As if, midst darkness, glimm'rings from above
Still point to sacred objects of our love.
Oh, would reality this vision chain,
And bind it fast till all its joys we gain ;
Or, if Hope's gone, no more to cheer our way,
And left us burdens to ourselves to stray,
Could we then but forget such visions seen,
And feed upon the present pastures green ?
E'en this poor boon is not our legacy,
Hope only leaves despair and misery.
Then farewell, phantom Hope, whose visions bright,
Have led through mazy scenes of all delight !
Enchanting, as they drew us with their bands,
But left us senseless on the desert sands.
Farewell the muse, for if sweet hope is fled,
Ambition and thy soul alike are dead !
Thy sweetest songs will now remain unsung,
Thy harp, with broken sound-board, lie unstrung.

THE WARBLER AND THE LILY;

OR,

PURITY AND THE MUSE.

TWO little Warblers perched upon
  Their lovely summer bowers,
Where round, in sweet profusion,
  Were scattered fragrant flowers.

" Now which of all those flowers," said one,
  " Wouldst thou have near thy nest ? "
" The Lily ; of all below the sun,
  I love the Lily best."

" Then come and sing her praise with me,"
  Said he, as off he flew ;
" Because of her spotless purity,
  I love the Lily too."

The Warbler, all disconsolate,
  Perched on his tree of old,
Though long he anxiously did wait,
  Her love she had not told.

"Is it because to other flowers
　A due respect I pay,
Or that thou to the genial showers
　Art wedded? Say, O say!

"Ah, Lily! Lily! speak one word,
　But say thou lovest me;
Thou'lt hear how I, a warbling bird,
　May grace the linden tree."

The Lily sweetly raised her head,
　And softly broke the spell,
While modestly she, whispering, said,
　"I've loved thee long and well."

Transported with delight was he,
　His light heart warmly beat;
Now soaring high he sang "Chee, chee,
　Chu-weetle-chu-weetle chu-weet."

Then back again to kiss her lip,
　Still moistened with the dew;
His loving song, "Chee-weep, chee-weep,
　A-teetle tee ta to-o-o."

Now, with still purer, nobler lays
　The joyous Warbler sings;
The fountains open up their sprays
　From hidden, living springs.

From every clime, of every hue,
   To join him in his song,
Sweet little feathered minstrels flew,
   And loud their notes prolong.

From every element now tribes
   Of every race are seen;
Their homage bring, and each subscribes
   To crown the Lily queen.

The fairies, with their goblets white,
   Pour incense at her feet;
And balmy zephyrs to unite,
   Bring blessings soft and sweet.

The nymphs of woods and waters came,
   With pearls to deck her brow;
For she is queen o'er all, they claim,
   Thus all to her should bow.

The rainbow, in the ambient air,
   Sheds her resplendent rays,
And promises no storm shall there
   Disturb her all her days.

All other flowers their fragrance bring,
   And grace the joyous scene;
With shouts the woods and welkin ring, —
   "*The Lily is our queen!*"

To yield the palm, the blushing rose,
    Delighted, sets her sail;
From us, from all, *decision* flows,
    Where Warblers once did fail.*

To this the modest new-made queen:
    "Alone I'd not endure;
To reign o'er such vast empire seen,
    All flowers alike are pure.

"Yet, since I'm chosen to preside,
    Let us together strive
All weeds, and venomed tribes that glide,
    From our domains to drive.

"That where the Warbler's notes are heard,
    Love, joy, and peace abound;
And purity the land shall gird
    With blessings all around."

MORAL.

Unhallowed strains may find a place,
    And vulgar minds amuse;
But purity alone can grace
    The warblings of the muse.

The pure in heart, the noble, great,
    Should love the humble muse,
And cheer with smiles to animate,
    Where naught his powers abuse.

* See Cowper's poem, "The Lily and the Rose."

THE LAVEROCK TO THE DAISY.

ART thou gone, whom I adore,
  Who could guide me on to duty;
Bloom'st thou now for me no more,
  Lovely flower of joy and beauty?
Is thy smile no more to cheer me,
Wilt thou never more be near me?

Or wilt thou, in other hours,
  Tell me still thy love is mine;
Needst thou but some April showers
  To reveal thy bright design?
Then, when I would perch me near thee,
Why do croakings bid me fear thee?

Why do rude winds blow between, —
  Withered leaves of weeping willows, —
So thy bloom cannot be seen,
  More than on the wild sea billows?
Know'st thou how they fill with sadness,
Driving me to scenes of madness?

Is it but the early dew
  That has closed and hid thy brightness ;
Will the sunshine ope anew,
  And reveal to me thy whiteness?
O, that I could know thy will !
For I love thee, love thee, still.

Tell me, sweet one, would thy smile
  Light me, if I build beside thee ;
Sweet'ning, while I pray the while,
  Naught but good may e'er betide thee ?
Wouldst thou share my humble dwelling,
When my heart for thee is swelling?

Or, if duty bids me soar
  To warble in the matin chorus ;
Tell me, pure one, I implore,
  Would thy beam still shine before us?
Tell me, would thy fragrance blessing
Answer to my notes caressing ?

Then might each our anthems raise,
  Through what meed to each is given ;
Thou to bloom, and I to praise,
  Glory to the God of Heaven.
Love and praise from earth and air,
Attributes from each our share.

A SINGLE RAINY DAY.

THROUGH waving fields and pastures green,
   With golden harvests gay,
A noble river once was seen
   To wend its living way.

One husbandman, with int'rest deep,
   Where'er it cast its spray,
Had charge o'er all its banks to keep
   Against each rainy day.

And thinking now the harvest white
   He soon should bear away,
Prepared, nor dreamed that all to blight
   Should come this rainy day.

Prepared to make each rough way plain,
   To level every brae,
In honest hope, all home to gain,
   Ere came a rainy day.

In eager hope, the reapers wait
   Another genial ray;
Alas! what now has changed their fate?
   A single rainy day.

The noble river, now enlarged,
    Resistless sweeps its way,
And through its banks the waves discharged
    That single rainy day.

But now, since all the farmer's hopes
    In desolation lay,
Does he to fate resign his crops,
    And curse this rainy day?

No; but his strength against the tide,
    And hope in Heaven he lays,
To heal the breaches thus made wide
    By sad and rainy days.

Should dark misfortune come to doom
    Our prospects to decay;
Take heart again; the deepest gloom
    Precedes the clearest day.

FRIENDSHIP'S WREATH.

DEAR friend of my youth, when fate bids us part,
  What humble gift would endure in your heart?
I'll twine you a wreath from some flowery grove,
And bind it around with strong cords of love.
A branch of the vine begins my sweet toil,
I'll round it lay moss and the cinquefoil;
That chastely blended, with that from above,
You may bask in rays of parental love.
With those in the wreath I will woodbine twine,
That fraternal joy unmix'd may be thine.
For daisy and crocus I'd wander miles,
That you may dwell with sweet innocent smiles.
Lucern and olive the store will increase,
May your life be long, its attendant peace.
And yet there is one sweet Southey has sung,
Around which earth's greatest blessings are hung;
Though sorrow it only may bring to me,
One shoot let there be from the linden tree;
And if you'll allow it, in some green spot,
Though small, yet a sprig of forget-me-not.

I 'll fence all round with the evergreen pine,
And sprinkle them o'er with dewdrops divine ;
That in kindness you 'll sometimes think of me,
However much joy with others you see.
With purity's sunshine your paths abound,
While all shed sweet-scented fragrance around.

AN EASTERN FARMER TO THE SHEPHERD

WHO HAS DESERTED HIS FLOCKS.

OH, wanderer, return !
    Back as the gentle dove,
Ere tempests crash the sacred urn,[*]
    'T is justice claims this evidence of love.

He who refused, yet went ;
    Did thus obedience prove.
So mayst thou come, ere day is spent —
    'T is love demands this evidence of love.

Return and feed thy flock,
    Nor ever from them rove ;
So when he sees thee on the rock,
    Faith will this hail, as evidence of love.

The day will soon be gone ;
    Soon darkness reign above ;
Haste, then, return, to this alone,
    Hope ling'ring clings, as evidence of love.

[*] Of love.

A PLEA FOR WORKING GIRLS.

STITCH! stitch! stitch!
  The burden once of a poet's song;
While the pay grew less, and the hours grew long,
Still the pale maid stitched her garments o'er,
To drive the ravenous wolf from the door.

  Dig! dig! dig!
The coolies' and negroes' weary sigh,
As their white oppressor raises on high
The lash, with oaths and an eye of fire,
That crushes in sorrow the rising ire.

  Weep! weep! weep!
For oppressive woes in other lands;
For the toiling, stitching, yet. starving bands;
For weak maids working by midnight lamp,
In desolate attics so cold and damp.

  Hark! hark! hark!
To the widow's and orphan girl's wail,
When oppression looms in the distant gale;
Ah, poverty's woes they dread far more
Than pestilence raging around their door!

Shame! shame! shame!
To the men — and for such let us search —
Who would prey upon souls, as pikes on perch,
Or pipers, who sound discordant tones,
And would feed their poor starving dogs on bones.

Wake! wake! wake!
Friends of humanity, hear the call!
Are not they worthy thy sympathy all,
Who honestly live by sweat and toil,
Who live by stitching, or turning the soil?

Speak! speak! speak!
From whence come some of our noblest wives,
Who cheer the laborers' homes and their lives?
Where does religion best workers find,
With loving hearts deep in their work enshrined?

No! no! no!
Not from the idle and dissolute trains,
Who neither have wit, affection, nor brains;
Nor midst the proud, the rich, or the great,
Whose aim 's to live in luxuriant state!

See! see! see!
They come from a noble, honored band,
Who faithfully trust their Creator's hand;
Who seek to walk in his love and fear,
Regardless of false society's sneer.

Woe! woe! woe!
To the man who would seek to degrade
The social sphere of the hard-working maid;
The end will come for oppressive care, —
There's a God who will hear the maiden's prayer!

Praise! praise! praise!
For a nation, whose flag can now wave
O'er a land that holds not a single slave!
Long may that banner float o'er the sea,
Flag of the prosperous, happy, and free!

LINES

WRITTEN FOR A BASKET OF SEA WEEDS AND SHELLS.

Y OU have found us deserted, alone on the beach,
  Where farthest the ocean's wild billows can reach ;
Neglected and torn from our home in the sea,
O, take us to shine in thy cottage with thee !

In that garden we grew o'er which briny waves flow,
And are only poor wrecks of the grandeur below ;
From the bright gems and flowers were we cast even now,
That have once decked the wreath on a mermaid's brow.

O ! care for the poor little waifs, cast on your shores,
Or who tearfully, timidly, knock at your doors ;
They are gems, they are pearls, to save or to drown ;
Then gently lift, prize them, they'll shine in your crown.

PARTING MOMENTS NIGH.

A SONG.

PARTING moments nigh,
  Wayward thoughts should vanish;
Let us therefore try
  All selfish will to banish.

Fleeting though they be,
  Few and fast decreasing,
Spent in happy glee,
  May yield a life-long blessing.

But cold lethargies
  Evermore may sever;
Little courtesies
  May knit fond hearts forever.

Longest lasts to view,
  Sunny retrospection;
Smiling, bid adieu!
  And keep the heart's affection.

Parting moments nigh,
   Wayward thoughts should vanish ;
Let us therefore try
   All selfish will to banish.

THE ROSE DELIGHTS AT EARLY MORN.

A SONG.

THE rose delights, at early morn,
Ere reapers come among the corn,
Its graceful head to bow and dip,
And kiss its neighbor's dewy lip.

Their green and tender bows entwine,
For strength and beauty while they shine;
Then, dying, fall the lovely pair,
Yet fragrance leave to scent the air.

Thus would I seek to kiss thee now,
And all my love for thee avow;
Thus would I tenderly embrace,
To shield from care, and help to grace.

And if with this thy love combined,
We'd bloom to cheer and bless mankind,
So living with unselfish aim,
Departing, leave a fragrant name.

FAREWELL TO SUNSHINE.

A SONG.

AIR: "The Last Rose of Summer."

'T IS the last ray of sunshine is fading away,
    From the broad swelling sea, where it danced on the
       spray;
Its last rosy hue has long died on the plain
Of the land that I love, and may ne'er see again.

Then adieu to the loved ones, so oft wont to meet
By the loud-sounding billow, or sylvan retreat;
No more by the clear winding rivers I'll roam,
For the Fates have forbid me to call this my home.

Thus the fond hopes we cherish in earlier days,
Will recede from our vision as friendship decays;
Yet new rays in pity will come to relieve,
Though 't is new scenes and friendships may deign to receive.

Then, oh, why should I murmur at duty's loud call!
I will bid you farewell, with a "God bless you all."
May *this* ray ne'er perish, — we'll meet and be blessed,
Where hope, in fruition, to the weary is rest.

(80)

LOVE AND MOONSHINE.

I 'LL take me away to her bower,
  And I 'll whisper, " Sweet maiden, I love ; "
I will earnestly plead in that hour,
  That she 'll be my own sweet turtle dove.
And if, by the *moon's pallid ray*,
  She should treat with cold distance my vow ;
I will cry, " 'T is a joke what I say,
  For I don't care a fig for you now."

But if to my suit she agree,
  And she say that she loves me all o'er,
How delighted and happy I 'll be,
  With what joy will my spirits now soar.
Ah, then, by the *moon's gentle beam*,
  I will clasp to my heart and caress ;
Both our lives will now pass like a dream,
  And I 'll kiss the sweet lips that said " Yes ! "

O then I will twine her a wreath,
  By the *moon's brilliant radiance*, I trow ;
From the mountain, the valley, and heath,
  And I 'll place it upon her fair brow.

6

Then off to the parson we 'll hie,
　While the moon *dances light o'er our head,*
And I 'll say, with a sweet little sigh,
　"Oh, dear!   Pray, sir, we want to get wed."

DAYLIGHT WOOING.

A SONG.

DARLING, I would come when daylight
    Drives the darkness far away ;
When no peering eyes in graylight,
    Take me for some bird of prey.
When the wood-bird, tick, tick, tapping,
    Beats the hollow linwood tree,
And the dew each flower is sapping,
    To perfume the greenwood lea.

Then I 'll rightly know the meaning,
    In thy smiles and sweet replies ;
With my soul, enraptured, gleaning
    Priceless treasures from thine eyes.
Or when huntsmen's horns are sounding,
    Hie we to the forest too,
Lightly through the wild woods bounding,
    Thus, ah, thus, I 'd love to woo !

IN ADVERSITY.

A SONG.

ALTHOUGH we may in darkness sit,
  And foul suspicions round us gather;
Although our powers may lose their wit,
  The wings of friendship many a feather.

Oh, say! can we still find *one* friend
  Whose faith will yet remain unshaken?
Whose sympathies with sorrows blend, —
  Thus all the cords of music waken?

Who will permit a hope to dwell
  Within the heart that still lies thirsting?
Who still of promised bliss will tell,
  When innocence the clouds are bursting?

FAREWELL SONG.

FAREWELL! farewell, thou lovely one,.
　　This burden I must carry,
To love, and yet to love alone,
　　Since thou refuse to tarry.

This heart will break, with every sound
　　Of joy, where'er I wander;
'T will mind me of the joy I found,
　　When aye my heart grew fonder.

Ah! what has stol'n thy heart away,
　　And made me thus so weary?
Not greater love! compare the ray
　　And find all others dreary.

Is pomp and state thy guiding star,
　　With Fortune's wheel to vary?
Another turn, the stately car
　　May change the scene so airy.

Farewell to song; since thou art gone,
　　Each chord I touch will languish, —
Ambition dead, each tune anon
　　Would show me born to anguish.

INTRODUCTION TO SHIRDENMEAD.

ON sweet Canadia's eastern plains,
  Enriched with gold and copper veins,
There stands, in a sequestered nook,
The lovely town of Shirdenbrook ;
Where Magog, like a sporting child,
Leaps over rocks and ridges wild,
And, in her freaks, drives many a wheel,
For sawing wood and grinding meal ;
Or turning shafts, without the vapor,
That Angus lays to make this paper ;
She kindly bids men save their steam,
Then, laughing, hides in Francis' stream.
Thus Nature, in her smallest plan,
Still laughs at mighty schemes of man.

 Invited by a genial squire,
I hastened thence with all desire.
"Mayhap," said he, "in country life,
You'll chase the deer or find a wife.
O'er hill and dale you're free to roam,
And taste of pleasures not at home.

Whatever best may suit your habits,
Though hunting fox or shooting rabbits,
Or if to minerals inclines
Your taste, then welcome to the mines!
But should the drizzly rain and cold
Combine to drive us from the wold,
You'll find a case of dead men's brains,
Of living authors and remains,
Where you may quaff exciting treason,
Or quietly have a feast of reason.
There's hist'ry, sacred or profane;
The way to endless peace or pain;
Some brilliant, new, or old translations,
Annals of poor, or wealth of nations;
In fact, you'll find within the store
What you may wish of any lore.
You then, when satisfied with books,
May find amusement dressing hooks;
Should this not suit your taste so well,
Then have a game at bagatelle."
A week, responsive to his call,
Paid merry tribute to them all,
When, on an afternoon, we strayed
To view a purchase he had made, —
A most romantic spot, indeed,
The small Estate of Shirdenmead;
Through which St. Francis' waters glide,
And kiss the verdure on each side;

With trees, beneath whose cooling shade
Delighted bathes the village maid.
That Autumn day the sky was clear,
Save when some fleecy clouds appear,
And move in undulating ways,
Like curling smoke in slanting rays.
No tongue can tell, no artist paint
The pastures green, the mourning plaint
Which echoed from the distant hills,
Through forest pines, o'er trickling rills.
The snow-white flocks in Eden pens,
Girt with the river, woods, and glens:
All Nature, sparkling with delight,
Seemed to foretell a peaceful night;
And in her gayest robes attired,
Our very inmost souls inspired
With holy feelings, and infuse,
Through all, the spirit of the muse.
Here, seated on a verdant mound,
And at our feet the fav'rite hound,
While on the stream's opposing brink
A noble stag had come to drink.
In centre of St. Francis' stream
There stands, as in a silent dream,
A huge, unchisell'd, boulder rock,
On which, defying tempest shock,
A one-side-blighted pine-tree waves,
While either side the current laves.

"How strange," said I, "it is to see
Grow on a barren rock a tree,
With no apparent kindly earth,
Or genial soil, to give it birth.
An emblem, to a certainty,
Of life, midst sore adversity.
Some tiny seed which summer's breeze
Has wafted from the forest trees,
Or tossed upon the winter's storm,
Has settled in a crevice warm.
There, watered by the gentle sprays,
And nursed by genial fruitful rays,
It germinates, it buds and blooms,
And still anon it strength assumes.
Its wants were few, else had it died,
For aught its scanty store supplied;
But now, its growing stem to save,
It seeks its food from wave to wave;
Or works its course down to the earth,
Below the rock that gave it birth.
Thus Childhood's happy hours are past,
With scarce a shadow o'er them cast,
When poor; yet blessed food and play,
Content beguiles the time away;
The rich enjoy no happier mood,
But are content with play and food.
O, happy Childhood! naught betrays
The sorrows of thy future days, —

The cares and toils, a ceaseless round,
And man to man unfaithful found.
The world around, the busy throng,
Is but to thee a pleasant song.
The hunter, leaping o'er the rill,
The humming, plashing, dusty mill,
Like murmuring waters as they roll,
But lend enchantment to thy soul,
And fill thy teeming fancies bright
With visions of some pure delight.
Of nymphs and fairies, who shall wait
On thee, when thou art high in state.
Too soon, alas! child of the poor,
You 'll beg your bread from door to door,
Or work your way in toil and sweat,
The scanty staff of life to get.
This last, a joy, if all were good,
But sad oppression may intrude ;
Or tongue of scandal wave on wave,
That hunts the needy to the grave ;
To drive thy fibres from the soil,
Where thou wouldst find reward for toil.
Yes ; toil is sweet with hope and love,
And faith in future joys above ;
But many like this tree are born,
To bear the yoke, oppressor's scorn ;
On all they do, to wear the blight,
Of words and deeds of men in might."

"Thy musings," said mine host, "recall
Some vivid pictures, wrought with gall,
Of tragic kinds, yet truthful scenes,
From which the village gossip gleans ;
A harvest rich as Francis' flow,
In tales of folly, pride, and woe!
And in them you may sadly trace
Connection with this very place.
But, see! the crimson sun goes down!
'T is late! The clouds that make him frown,
And shades around his ancient. form,
Give indications of a storm.
The scenes, if nothing worthier hail,
May grace an after-supper tale."

THE ANGEL OF MERCY TO CHICAGO.

WE 'VE heard of thy sad desolation,
    What misery firebrands have sown ;
We hasten to speak consolation,
    And make all thy sorrows our own.

Arise from thine ashes, Chicago !
    From smouldering ruins and flame ;
The Angel of Mercy's embargo
    Prohibits oblivion's shame.

Too dear to us all were the favors
    Religion and commerce received ;
Thy bounty, with sweet-smelling savors,
    The hungry and thirsty relieved.

All cities have sins and have sorrows ;
    Were none of those sins thine own ?
Shun all from which misery borrows,
    And vile *Speculation* disown.

Arise, then, a purified city,
   And where thou wast greatest in fame
Be greatest in love and in pity, —
   And light to poor heathens proclaim.

That so from thy radiant centre
   The name of the Saviour still sound ;
All lands shall return with the censer,
   To sprinkle thee blessings around.

WITHIN A DELL.

A SONG.

WITHIN a dell,
    That I love well,
There lives a maiden I love better;
    Amidst the swell,
    Who, can you tell,
Will bear that lovely one a letter?

    By your breeding,
    Sure the reading
Is not for you, but for another;
    Anxious speeding,
    Though with pleading,
Be ye father, friend, or brother.

    A deep blue eye,
    Not very high,
Her hair is waving, fair, and racy;
    Whilst moments fly,
    I 'll wait reply
From her who bears the name of Gracie.

RELIGIOUS POEMS.

ODE TO TIME.

O TIME! most princely gift of all earth's train,
   God has, in mercy infinite, left with man.
Without thy bliss, none else would be enjoyed ;
But with thee, aids of Heaven may be employed.
Thy little moments, though of smallest measure,
Each worth a mine of brilliant, glitt'ring treasure.
What idlers, by their vain, intrusive stay,
Steal from us, and, in stealing, throw away,
Thou brief soul's respite ! in whose less'ning space
We're loudly called to seek for saving grace.
What man, with this in view, with actions rude,
With idle dreams, or slumb'ring eyelids, would
Kill time while active reason holds the throne,
Or squander what he cannot call his own ?
Which past, no power on earth can e'er recall,
Or substitution find we, search through all ;
Or, if once lost, can never more be found,
Though search be made the universe around.
Yet Time, in his triumphant march, sweeps on,
Nor stops ; but while the sluggard sleeps, is gone.
Nor waits unthinking loiterers' tardy feet,
If pace with him they'd keep, they must be fleet.

7

Thou boon for which the debtor humbly craves,
For which the dying sinner madly raves,
Who, in his life, had from him anxious hurled,
Would now, to stay thy fleetness, give the world ;
Though, through his life, the infidel deny,
Now cannot hide, but tells, with piteous eye,
As he is found, thy period outrun,
Immutable Eternity's begun.
Come, buoyant youth, whilst yours to use he is,
Through all your joys, behold how he, in his
Majestic stride, and independent sway,
Will never take a favor without pay.
We cannot call him an ungrateful knave ;
Save him, and find how much to you he 'll save ;
Improve him, and yourself will be improved ;
Love him, and find yourself the more beloved.
But call him enemy, misuse, or hate —
Thyself will suffer, perishing ingrate ;
For injury to him so sure must bring
At last, to conscience, a remorseless sting.
He drinks the blessedness of which we sing,
And call our own ; or, with his love-tipped wing,
Dispels the shadows of the darkest night,
And hidden depths of darkness brings to light.
Gives joy, the sorrow-laden to assume,
Or villains with their projects casts in gloom ;
Turns peace to war, and war again to peace ;
The frail and tott'ring monarch's strength increase,

Or strongest kingdoms to their base will shake,
And happy homes a desolation make.
Makes princes beggars, they with princes mate ;
Born in a hovel, man may lie in state ;
Or, fanned and nurtured in the lap of ease,
Within his reach all comforts man can please,
May die a wretched vagrant in thy span,
Forsaken both alike by God and man.
Time smiling nature casts in winter's gloom,
And with the snow, lays down in living tomb ;
But, though the darkness loom, each circling spring
Makes flowers to bloom anew, and linnets sing.
To life brings teeming myriads untold,
And unto dust again turns young and old.
In truth, he worketh wonders all the way,
In great designs of blossom and decay.
O young man, wake ! thy influence is vast ;
Seize each fleet moment's blessings, ere they 've past,
And store them all up as he onward flies,
With outstretched finger, pointing to the skies.
Have you abused the past, and injured him ?
In present and future redeem the time.
With deeds of holiness and truth begin,
Your life to crown, and others lead from sin.
In each, thus led to Jesus you 'll enjoy
Another life, and bliss without alloy.
Time thus improved and ended, — Heaven begun,
Enjoy eternal many Heavens in one.

A DREAM.

ONE smiling morn, reclining on my bed,
    And weary nature's refuge almost fed ;
My eyelids closed, sweet sleep to satiate,
While thoughts, intent on time expatiate.
A vision drew my senses as I lay,
And bore me hence, in dreams from earth away ;
The clouds in crimson, purple, and in red,
Were seen with variegated colors shed ;
Through all, chained lightnings livid glimm'rings played,
With lines of gold and silver there inlaid.
Behind, the moon stood pale, and stars aghast,
When, lo ! a sound as of a trumpet's blast ;
And Luna, burst to many moons, did seem
With hues unmentioned here, I saw in dream.
In silent tumults, all the air did rend ;
The stars and planets down in showers descend.
Again a sound, as bomb in battle's rear,
Its echo bursting on the distant ear.
And voices cry, " Look ! look ! what sights appear !
O wondrous view ! O sight to memory dear !
Even space itself looked pale, and, reft in twain,
By music sweet and of angelic strain,
Made way for something floating through the air ;
And, drawing near, revealed a city fair,

With white and glist'ning palaces in line,
Sailing o'er oceans, as of love divine,
Until it me enveloped, as I stood,
And there, in glory, I in raptures viewed
A clear, bright city, of celestial kind,
Such never was conceived by human mind.
Its streets of gold, gates, walls of pearly white,
With mansions pure, and filled with radiant light ;
O'er which bright seraphs, with their trumpets, fly,
And fill it with sweet strains of music high.
In midst of it a great and pure white throne ;
On Him, who sat thereon, a jewelled crown ;
His countenance transparent as the light,
And brighter than the sun in all his might,
Such lustrous splendors all his form pervade ;
Such glowing brightness that shall never fade ;
That even through his robes, which sparkling gleam,
The rays of light with dazzling brightness stream.
Such companies of saints the holiest fill,
And angels bend their wings to do his will.
The Saviour's dying love their constant theme,
Uniting each to all, and all to Him.
And every saint and angel, every thing and place,
Reflective shed the brightness of his face.
O scenes immortal ! O ecstatic joy !
Such strains of music ne'er did harp employ.
I wondering stood, to scenes like this unused,
And meditative on the theme I mused,
While seraphs raised anew their joyous hymn,
Sweet voices whisper, 't is the end of time.

ADDRESS TO A BEREAVED YOUNG LADY.

'TWAS yesterday, the time called vesper,
    My ears were summoned by a whisper, —
A whisper wafted across the seas;
The sigh of sadness was on that breeze.
Forgiveness I crave, that now I should
On sorest bereavement thus intrude;
But every pang that rends thy heart
Must deep on my bosom leave a smart.
Oh, deny me not to mingle here,
With you a tributary tear!

    Merciful father, incline thine ear,
While to thy footstool ascends this prayer:
Soothe her deep sorrow, Thou great " I am,"
Oh, "temper the wind to this shorn lamb";
Touch with thy finger the wound, and heal;
Lift up this veil, and thy love reveal.

    Those severed ties that have bound to earth,
But show new traits of a Saviour's worth;
For there, in that land of love divine,
A gem in His crown, behold him shine!

Is earth made lonely by treasure transferred ?

'T is that the place where he 's gone be preferred ;

And Jesus weeps, as at Lazarus' grave ;

Wept not that Himself must die to save,

Nor weeps He for him to glory taken,

But weeps with her who with grief is stricken.

In sympathy weeps, yet in love reveals,

It is for her good that thus He deals ;

To the realms of bliss He hath taken this one,

That her heart more close to his own be drawn.

Then weep not for him, just sighed to rest,

He but reclines on a Saviour's breast ;

Yet, since we must his absence endure,

We 'll nurse sweet thoughts of the meek and pure,

And aye in thy heart enbalméd be,

His loved and unsullied memory.

SEEK JESUS.

A GOSPEL MINISTER'S DYING CHARGE TO HIS CHILDREN.

IN solemn hour of dissolution, lies
    A faithful minister of God, and wise ;
Who breathes to those around him, ere he dies,
          Seek Jesus ! Seek Jesus !

Oft had those sweet, inviting words been said,
And oft the spirit's rays around them shed ;
While with his flock he earnestly had plead,
          Seek Jesus ! Seek Jesus !

Unconscious, — still his lingering spirit stayed,
Till by his side his little child is laid ;
His weeping friends still think of what he bade,
          Seek Jesus ! Seek Jesus !

An instant, consciousness returns ; he smiled,
And fixed his eyes upon his darling child ;
Expiring, faintly said, in accents mild,
          Seek Jesus ! Seek Jesus !

That voice is now forever hushed, and he
Gone to his mansion in eternity.
But list! the child now answers wond'ringly,

Seek Jesus! Seek Jesus!

From her, a younger still the words up caught,
Who, silently, the youngest babe now sought,
And lisped those words the dying father taught,

Seek Jesus! Seek Jesus!

Now hark ye what is heard from day to day,
From room to room, and even at their play,
In whispers earnestly they, lisping, say,

Seek Jesus! Seek Jesus!

From babes and sucklings God doth perfect praise;
Then let us listen to the hymn they raise,
And join with them in solemn, earnest lays,

Seek Jesus! Seek Jesus!

While in the business of our lives each day,
Be this the greatest part of all to say
In loving whispers, to all those who stray,

Seek Jesus! Seek Jesus!

The spirit and the bride unite to call;
Let him that heareth, leave each sinful thrall,
And echo forth to him that thirsts to all,

Seek Jesus! Seek Jesus!

Unfathomable source of love and grace!
Help us to lead our friends to seek thy face,
And may those words descend from race to race,
        Seek Jesus! Seek Jesus!

THE BELIEVER'S CONFLICT AND VICTORY.

HOW can I tell the inward strife
    That brought me from the jaws of Death?
How can I speak the matchless love
    That wrought in me a living faith?

With doubt and fear, my guilty soul
    Was tossed upon a troubled sea;
The waves of wrath against me roll;
    To sin, the tempter tempted me.

I sought to turn from error's ways,
    To look where mercy is revealed;
But Satan loud the cry did raise,
    "Your sins are more than can be healed.

"Too oft you have dishonored God;
    Your guilty soul to dust will cleave;
You've trampled under foot His blood,
    And nothing now can you relieve."

In my own strength I did prepare,
    Of sin to gain the conquest o'er;
But Satan caught me in his snare,
    And tempted me to sin the more.

I sought, for counsel, men of God,
   Who would their own experience tell;
They bade me fear the chast'ning rod,
   And made me more the child of hell!

Thus lost, in guilt and sin I lay,
   In darkness and in misery;
Without one cheering hopeful ray,
   Lost! Lost! for all eternity.

Wounded and weak, *God's Word* I sought,
   His precious promises to man;
The *breath of Heaven* around me wrought
   Salvation's wondrous plan.

For near me now the *Saviour* drew,
   And filled my soul with radiant light;
His head was wet with early dew;
   His locks with droppings of the night.

His wounded hands and feet he showed,
   His piercéd side, His thorn-crowned brow;
He said, *for you* I bore this load,
   O, faithless one, believe me now.

Long had He waited at the door,
   His bowels with compassion moved;
No words of chiding did He pour,
   But tender love and mercy proved.

He had a balm for every wound,
  A pardon for my guiltiness;
He me with peace and honor crowned,
  And clothed me with his righteousness.

MEDITATIONS IN A BURYING-GROUND.

ONE Summer eve, faint, weary, worn;
　　My heart with grief oppressed;
I sat me down upon a grave
　　To seek some mental rest.

The moon, set in a watery sky,
　　Beam'd through the watery trees,
Whose silken, rustling sound anon,
　　Sighed gently o'er the breeze.

And oft the sound of heavy drops
　　Would fall upon my ears,
As if Heaven vied with friends to weep,
　　And sprinkle all with tears.

The shadow of each stone erect
　　O'er every grave was spread,
Like forms from spirit land, who watch
　　The ashes of the dead.

Then listen! giddy, thoughtless crowds,
　　On wings of pleasure borne;
Learn from these graves, and nature too,
　　That man must often mourn.

Solemn or careless wanderers,
  O'er graves and tombstones pause,
Ye who in faith attend and keep,
  Or set aside God's laws.

Each silent inmate, if he could,
  Would raise his head and warn,
To flee for refuge to the Rock,
  We now so treat with scorn.

One parched with thirst, the drop denied,
  Would say, "Go, tell my friends,
O, while in life prepare for death!
  Beyond — no grace extends."

One, who in life had sought the Lord,
  And trusted in his grace,
Would tell the wonders of His love,
  And beauty of His face;

How hills dissolved with drops of blood,
  Each barrier downward cast;
How footsteps sipp'd the swelling flood,
  And led to heaven at last.

But silence reigns! no storms disturb,
  Nor varying seasons change;
No faithless hopes can lead astray,
  No doubts or cares derange.

Here all is mute! nor joy is heard,
　Nor sighs, nor fears, nor groans.
Then read some lessons from the graves,
　Some wisdom from the stones.

For often yet will Christ appear,
　And softly breathe their name
To those who seek Him at the grave,
　As He to Mary came.

The high, the low, the rich, the poor,
　The lettered and unlearned,
All mingle here in common clay,
　Respecter none's discerned.

Here one, who, living for this earth,
　Had sought the praise of men,
Forgetful of humility,
　When in this lonely glen;

And glorified by millions round,
　For every word and plan —
But having aimed to live a god,
　He yet must die a man.

Here is a monument of sense,
　In marble, pure and white;
Whilst happ'ly fitted for this place,
　Its words and acts unite.

On top, a lovely form is seen,
  With finger raised on high,
And with a sweet, benignant smile,
  Attracts the passer-by.

There, by her side, the anchor Hope
  Cheers fainting, downcast men ;
And o'er it hangs a sacred scroll,
  Says, " We shall meet again."

A little farther on we move,
  It will this verify :
A little marble marks the spot
  Where all a family lie.

A little infant, three days old ;
  The mother died in prime ;
The father, a ripe shock of corn,
  Had mourned through ample time.

What ailed thee, babe, that thou so soon
  Shouldst cast off earth's restraint ?
Thou but hast waited long enough
  To gain the name of saint.

Without the taste of bitterness,
  With which this life is fraught,
Partaker of the benefits,
  Redeeming love hath bought.

8

Ah, three days! yes, the Saviour there,
  In gloomy grave did lie:
He stooped to fight the conqueror,
  And now even death must die.

MERCY AT ZION'S GATE.

A HYMN.

O, HOW divinely sweet,
　　To come to Zion's Gate;
To bow, in faith, at mercy's feet,
　　To pray, to praise and wait.

O, Lord, inspire our souls
　　With greater love to Thee!
Thy mercy, as the heaven, rolls
　　O'er every land and sea.

Before Thee, here we stand,
　　Deserving naught but ill,
But mercy offers us the hand
　　Of love and blessing still.

O, grant us, of Thy grace!
　　To hear aright the voice;
This offered mercy to embrace:
　　And in Thy love rejoice!

FATHER AND SON;

OR,

PRAYER ANSWERED IN ADVERSITY.

———

FROM morning until noon,
   A tender father chides his erring child;
In faith assured, that soon
   He'll hear an answer to his accents mild.

That son the downward way
   Departs still farther from his father's home,
And, blighting every ray,
   Heaps injuries that swell like surging foam.

Night closing o'er him fast,
   The father homeward, sternly, sadly turns;
Yet, thinking of the past,
   A yearning to forgive within him burns.

The tempest rages high:
   He stops! 't is like the voice, "Father, forgive!"
Or but the wind's wild sigh.
   He waits to see the face if yet he live.

Days, nights in anguish past,
  Yet not a sound from him he sought to save;
Grief hath death's shadow cast
  O'er him. He sinks in sorrow to the grave.

Yet hear the prayer of Faith,
  That rises higher from that sinking frame:
"Save! save! from endless death,
  My son, O God, I ask, in Jesus' name!"

Full many a winter's storm
  Had spent its fury o'er that lonely tomb,
Since fell that noble form:
  Sweet flowers had shed full many a summer's bloom.

When, at the close of day,
  Some wand'rers near the village heard a groan,
And peering in the gray,
  Beheld once more that father's only son.

Long did he live to grieve
  O'er all the past; to mourn a father lost;
But yet in Faith believe,
  And find a Saviour henceforth all his boast.

ISAIAH, CHAPTER LI.

I.

GIVE ear ye that love righteousness,
  And ye that seek the Lord;
Look to the rock whence ye were hewn,
  And called by His Word.

II.

To Abraham, your Father, look,—
  To Sarah, and adore;
For him I called alone and blest;
  Yea, and increased in store.

III.

For God shall comfort Zion yet;
  Yea, all her places waste;
Her wilderness like Eden make.
  With gardens sweetly grac'd.

IV.

Even like the garden of the Lord,
  Her deserts shall rejoice,
And gladness shall be found therein,
  With praise and thankful voice.

V.

Hearken, my people, unto me,
  And, O my nation, hear!
A law shall from my mouth proceed,
  My judgment shall be clear.

VI.

My righteousness is near, and my
  Salvation forth is gone;
The Isles shall wait on thee, and they
  Mine arm shall trust upon.

VII.

Lift up your eyes unto the heavens,
  And see the earth beneath,
Like garments old the earth shall wax,
  Heaven vanish as a wreath.

VIII.

And they that dwell therein shall die,
  In manner like them sure;
Established shall my righteousness,
  And saving strength endure.

IX.

Hear me, ye that know righteousness,
  In whose heart is my law;
Fear not the vile reproach of men,
  When they their weapons draw.

X.

Like garments, moths shall eat them up,
  Worms shall them eat like wool;
But my salvation shall endure,
  My righteousness shall rule.

XI.

Awake! awake! put on thy strength,
  O arm of God, the Lord!
Awake! as in the ancient days,
  In generations ward!

XII.

Art thou not it, hath Rahab cut
  The Dragon wounded sore?
Art thou not it hath dried the sea,
  Deep waters run no more?

XIII.

That for thy ransomed people made
  The mighty deeps a wall,
To Zion, singing, shall return,
  The Lord's redeeméd all.

XIV.

And everlasting joy shall be
  Upon their heads, each one;
Gladness and joy shall they obtain,
  'Tis even now begun.

XV.

Sorrow and mourning from them shall
  Forever flee away.
I, even I, am he, the Lord
  That comforteth your way.

XVI.

Who then art thou, that thou shouldst fear
  A man that soon must die?
Or dread the son of man that shall,
  As grass be made to lie?

XVII.

The Lord, thy Maker, thou forgett'st,
  That stretched forth the Heaven:
Yea, who the earth's foundations laid,
  And strength to them hath given;

XVIII.

And thou hast feared continually
  Each day oppressor's might?
Where is the fury of the man
  That would oppress the right?

XIX.

The captive Exile hasteneth,
  That he may loosed be;
And that he should not die in pit,
  Nor failing stores may see.

XX.

But I'm the Lord, thy God, that did
  The sea divide and tame,
Whose furious waves have wildly roared, —
  The Lord of Hosts his name.

XXI.

And in thy mouth I've put my word,
  And covered thee, have I,
In shadow of mine hands, that I
  May plant the heavens high.

XXII.

And that I may, in righteousness,
  The earth's foundations lay;
And unto Zion's daughters all,
  Thou art my people, say.

XXIII.

Awake! awake! put on thy strength,
  O thou Jerusalem!
Which hast, at God's hands, drunk the cup
  Of fury full to brim;

XXIV.

For now thou drunken hast the dregs,
  Even to the very last,
The cup of trembling, and of wrath, —
  My fury now is past.

XXV.

'Mong all the sons whom she brought forth,
  She none to guide hath found,
Nor do the sons whom she brought up,
  With love to her abound.

XXVI.

These things, are they not come to thee?
  Who'll sorry for thee be?
Destruction, famine, and the sword,
  Who then shall comfort thee?

XXVII.

Thy sons lie fainting in the street,
  As wild bulls in a net;
Their fall, the fury of the Lord,
  And God's rebuke they get.

XXVIII.

Therefore, afflicted, hear ye this,
  Ye drunk, but not with wine!
For thus doth say thy Lord, the Lord,
  And thy God, even thine, —

XXIX.

That of His people pleads the cause,
  Behold! out of thy hand,
I have the cup of trembling drawn,
  Thou shalt before me stand.

XXX.

Even of my fury's cup the dregs,
  Thou to the last didst drain,
I 'll put in the hands of those,
  That thee afflict and pain ;

XXXI.

That to thy soul have said, "Bow down,
  That over we may go " ;
As ground thou hast thy body laid,
  As street to them also.